DOGS DON'T WEAR SNEAKERS

DOGS DON'T WEAR SNEAKERS

BY LAURA NUMEROFF
ILLUSTRATED BY JOE MATHIEU

ALADDIN PAPERBACKS
New York London Toronto Sydney

ALADDIN PAPERBACKS
An imprint of Simon & Schuster Children's Publishing Division
1230 Avenue of the Americas, New York, NY 10020
Text copyright © 1993 by Laura Numeroff
Illustrations copyright © 1993 by Joe Mathieu
Also available in a Simon & Schuster Books for Young Readers hardcover edition.
Designed by Vicki Kalajian
The text of this book was set in 20-point ITC Esprit Book.
The illustrations were done in pencil and dyes.
Manufactured in China
First Aladdin Paperbacks edition September 1996
Second Aladdin Paperbacks edition January 2005
2 4 6 8 10 9 7 5 3
The Library of Congress has cataloged the hardcover edition as follows:
Numeroff, Laura Joffe.
Dogs don't wear sneakers / by Laura Numeroff; illustrated by Joe Mathieu.
p. cm.
Summary: In a child's imagination, animals do wacky things, including
ducks riding bikes, yaks skiing, and fish eating bagels.
1. Animals—Juvenile poetry. 2. Children's poetry—American.
[1. Animals—Poetry. 2. Imagination—Poetry. 3. American poetry.]
1. Mathieu, Joseph, ill. II. Title. PS3564.U45D63 1993
811'.54—dc20 92-27007
ISBN 0-671-79525-2 (hc.)
ISBN 0-689-87828-1 (pbk.)

To Peanuts, Muffin, and Mandy
L.N.

To my mom, Patricia Mathieu
J.M.

Dogs don't wear sneakers

And pigs don't wear hats

And dresses look silly
On Siamese cats.

Sheep don't take showers
And goats never shave

And you won't find a bathtub
Inside a bear's cave.

Moose don't go bowling

And hens never swim

And you'll never see roosters
Working out in a gym.

Skunks don't ride scooters

And beavers don't skate

And frogs don't take cabs
When they're out on a date.

Cows don't go dancing

And yaks never ski

And you won't find a honey bun
Baked by a bee.

Fish don't eat bagels

And penguins don't teach

And rabbits don't sunbathe
At your local beach.

Now just close your eyes
And draw with your mind.
You might be surprised
At what you will find...

Like parrots in tutus

And lambs selling shoes

And two-story houses
Constructed by gnus,

Or mules painting pictures

And ducks riding bikes

And raccoons with knapsacks
On holiday hikes,

Or bulls flying airplanes

And snails saving twine.

But tell me what you see? It's your dream—not mine!